The Search for Autumn

Based on the characters, art, and stories created by Judith Hope Blau

By Judith Hope Blau and Ellie O'Ryan
Illustrated by Paul E. Nunn

Grosset & Dunlap

AMERICAN
FORESTS
americanforests.org

A portion of the proceeds of the sale of this book goes to American Forests to help plant trees for forest ecosystem restoration.

The publisher does not have any control over and does not assume any responsibility for author or third-party websites or their content.

Library of Congress Cataloging-in-Publication Data is available.

ISBN 978-0-448-45057-5   10 9 8 7 6 5 4 3 2 1

The Treetures are tiny magical creatures. They live inside a big oak tree in the middle of an enchanted forest in a place called Nutley Grove. Treetures care for trees all over the world. In this story, these tree keepers are getting ready for fall. The Mudsters are planning their Winter Feast and the young Sproutlings can't wait to see Autumn visit the forest. She always brings wonderful surprises for everyone! For more about the Treetures visit www.treetures.com.

Here are the Mudsters you'll meet in this book:

Mud Meister

Mud Meister is a Soil Spoiler.

Humus

Humus is a Super Compost Chef.

Crud

Crud is a Decayer.

Fun Gus

Fun Gus is a Mushroominator.

Root Snoot

Root Snoot is a Root Rotter.

Here are the Treetures you'll meet in this book:

Twigs is the
Treeture Teacher.

Blossom is a
Tree Twirler.

Sprig is a
Treedom Fighter.

Rootie and Roothie are Rooters.

Chlorophyll and Chlorophyllis
are part of the Sunbeam Team.

Woody and Phloemina
are Sap Tappers.

Stomper is a
Compost Master.

Mama Greenleaf is the
Keeper of the Crown.

Autumn is a
Leaf Turner.

Chip, Petals, and Pod are
Sproutlings.

It was a sunny day in Nutley Grove.
The Sproutlings were playing
hide-and-seek.
"Ready or not, here I come!"
yelled Chip.

A cool wind blew through the trees.
Leaves fluttered to the ground.
"Look, this leaf has yellow polka dots
on it," shouted Petals.
"Something is happening," said Pod.
"Let's ask Twigs about it."

The Sproutlings found Twigs at the Great Oak. "Why does this leaf have yellow dots on it?" asked Petals.

"Why is the weather cooler?" asked Chip.

"Why are the leaves falling?" asked Pod.

"Because Autumn is coming!" Twigs said.
"In our forest, many trees will lose their leaves.
But Autumn brings us a special surprise to take
their place!"

"We can't wait," said Pod.

"Let's go find Autumn!" said Chip.

Chlorophyll and Chlorophyllis, from the
Sunbeam Team, were outside with Sprig.
"We just came to say good-bye,"
Chlorophyll said.
"Autumn is almost here—so we're following
the summer birds to a sunny vacation spot!"

"The leaves use sunshine to make food for the tree.
That's called *photosynthesis*
(say it like: foh-toh-**sin**-thuh-sis).
When we go away, the green goes, too!
Then the leaves show their true colors.
When the leaves fall off, the tree stops making
food until spring," explained Chlorophyllis.
"We'll see you again when the new leaves grow!"

"Don't be sad, Sproutlings," said Sprig.
"They'll be back in the spring.
But now, the whole forest is getting ready for
Autumn! Would you like to help?"
"Yes!" cheered Chip, Petals, and Pod.

"Great!" Sprig said. "Let's see if Mama Greenleaf needs any help. She is one of the busiest Treetures when Autumn comes around!"

Mama Greenleaf was at the top of the tree.
"Hello, my little Sproutlings," she said.
"It's time to say good-bye to the leaves.
They seal off their stems to keep water and
food in the tree. This will help the leaves
grow again next spring."

The Sproutlings waved good-bye to the leaves as, one by one, they fluttered to the forest floor.

"Now let's go to the nursery to see the new baby Treetures," Mama Greenleaf said.

"Baby Treetures are born when acorns fall off the Great Oak," she said.

Little cradles were lined up in a row.

There was a baby Treeture in each one!

"Next spring, they'll be Sproutlings,
ready to learn all about trees—
just like you," whispered Mama Greenleaf.
"But until then, they need lots of love and care."

Then Mama Greenleaf showed everyone
her big project.

"Every year, when Autumn comes, I sew
fallen leaves together to make a blanket for
the forest floor.

That will help keep the roots warm, all winter
long," she explained.

"Rootie and Roothie also take care of the roots," Sprig said.

"Let's see if they need some help."

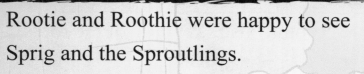

Rootie and Roothie were happy to see
Sprig and the Sproutlings.

"Can you help us cover the roots?" Rootie asked.

"Sure!" replied Pod.

"We need to put some leaves and twigs near the
roots," Roothie added.

Stomper ran over to join them. "That's when I come along to crush the leaves and twigs to make mulch," said Stomper.

The Sproutlings liked the sound of marching over the dry leaves.

"Great job!" Roothie said. "The crushed leaves and twigs will turn into new soil. That will be good tree food in the spring."

Nearby, Sprig and the Sproutlings found another busy Treeture—Blossom.

"Look at all the nuts and fruit!" she said. "Last spring, they started as tiny flowers that helped seeds grow. They've grown into yummy treats. And now it's time to harvest them!"

NORTHERN OAK

"Now the animals and birds will have lots of food to last the whole winter! And the seeds inside the fruit will make new trees for our forest," Blossom said.

Petals peeked into a hole in a tree—
inside she found Woody and Phloemina.
"Well, hello, little Sproutlings!" Phloemina said.
"We're getting the vessels in the trees ready for
winter. Vessels are like pipes that run through
the whole tree."

"With the right ingredients, the vessels will harden—but they won't freeze. Then, in the spring, they will bring food and water to all the parts of the tree!" said Woody.

Sprig and the Sproutlings walked on until they met the Mudsters! They looked very busy.

"No time to talk, Sproutlings," said Fun Gus.

"We need to gather all of the fallen leaves and twigs," he said.

Humus licked his lips. "Yum!"

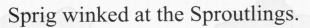

Sprig winked at the Sproutlings.
"While the Mudsters have their Winter Feast,
they'll also turn the leaves and twigs
into healthy soil!" he said.
"That will help *all* the plants in Nutley Grove
grow bigger and better than ever."

"Phew!" said Sprig.

"There is so much to do to get ready for Autumn."

"But *where* is Autumn?" asked Pod.

"We've been waiting and waiting, and Autumn *still* isn't here!"

Petals looked worried.

"What if Autumn doesn't come?" she asked.

"What would happen to Nutley Grove
without Autumn?"

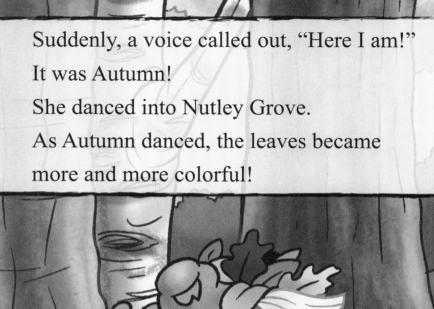

Suddenly, a voice called out, "Here I am!"
It was Autumn!
She danced into Nutley Grove.
As Autumn danced, the leaves became
more and more colorful!

"I see that all the Treetures have worked hard
to get the forest ready for the cold winter,"
Autumn said.

"And now for your special surprise—a Fall
Fair for everyone to enjoy!" shouted Autumn.

At the Fall Fair, there was a Leaf-Go-Round and a Canopy Coaster high in the trees. And there was bark climbing and root-scooter rides. Stomper led the Mulch March through all of Nutley Grove.

The Sproutlings had so much fun!
And on that magic day, all of the
Treetures' green hearts turned to gold—
one of Autumn's favorite colors.

After the fair, the Sproutlings snuggled
under their warm and cozy blankets.
Everyone in Nutley Grove was ready
for a long winter sleep.
Except the Mudsters—
their Winter Feast was just beginning!